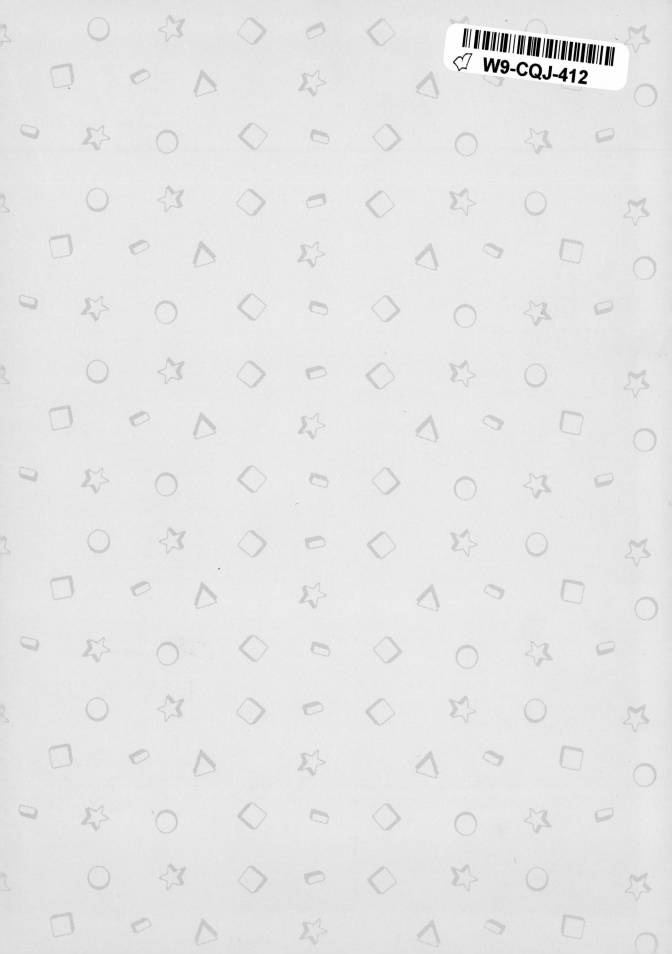

MICKEY'S
BEACH VACATION
A Book About Words

By Cindy West
Illustrated by Guell

A GOLDEN BOOK • NEW YORK
Western Publishing Company, Inc., Racine, Wisconsin 53404

A B C D E F G H I J K L M

van

map

One beautiful summer day Mickey and his friends were getting ready to leave for their vacation. "I'm so glad we're going to the beach," said Minnie. "I can't wait to jump into the cool blue ocean!"

"Are you sure it's a good idea for Goofy to do the driving?" asked Morty. "He's reading the map upside down!"

"Goofy's a good driver," Mickey assured him.

And in no time at all they were off.

haystack

hitching
post

vest

rope

boot

fence

saddle

mane

hat

spurs

horse

reins

Goofy drove the car east. "I'm sure the beach is this way," he said. "See, here's a sandy road!" Goofy drove the car down the sandy road…straight to a big dude ranch!

"This sure doesn't look like the beach," said Mickey. "But it *does* look like a lot of fun! Why don't we all stay here tonight?"

So they did. Mickey and Minnie went on an exciting horseback ride while Morty, Ferdie, and Goofy learned how to throw a lasso. "Yahoo!" Goofy hollered as he almost lassoed a hitching post.

The next morning Goofy made a promise to his friends. "We'll get to the beach by lunchtime," he said. "The map says it's just a little north of here."

Goofy drove on. But instead of finding the sandy beach, the friends wound up in the woods.

"We might as well stop and have lunch here," Minnie said. "I can pick some berries for dessert."

Morty and Goofy played hide-and-seek while Ferdie ran off to watch the deer.

bird

squirrel

deer

nest

bush

berries

grass

flowers

tree

stream

frog

owl

moon

branch

cup

tent

guitar

campfire

rock

plate

sleeping bag

"It's too late to go to the beach now," Mickey said when they were through eating. "Why don't we spend the night right here? I always keep some camping equipment in the van."

So Mickey gathered wood and built a big fire, which he surrounded with rocks for safety. "It's a good thing we brought plenty of food," said Ferdie.

"Especially marshmallows!" added Morty.

That night Minnie played a happy song on her guitar and everyone sang along.

swing

slide

skateboard

skate

bench

balloon

bike

seesaw

The next morning Mickey and the others packed up the van and drove back down the road. "I hear laughter coming from this direction!" said Morty as he pointed south.

"And I hear lots of activity!" yelled Goofy. "This time I'm *sure* we're heading toward the beach."

But instead they found themselves approaching a town with a very big playground!

"We went the wrong way *again*!" Ferdie groaned.

"We can still have a good time!" Goofy told him. "I'm going to take a ride on this seesaw!" Goofy sat himself down on the seesaw and waited for it to go.

"You can't ride a seesaw by yourself!" Ferdie said with a chuckle. "Morty and I will ride with you."

"This *is* much better!" Goofy agreed.

"Now let's go straight to the beach," said Minnie.

"It must be even farther south of here," said Goofy. "All the cars are heading that way!"

So they followed the long, long line of cars—and drove straight into a big city!

Morty and Ferdie groaned, "We'll never get to the beach."

"We have plenty of time to get there," Minnie told them. "But we should stay here tonight. Big cities are so exciting!"

pigeon

train

parking meter

bus

subway

shower

curtain

clock

tub

soap

lamp

telephone

bed

television

rug

picture

dresser

pillow

table

stool

Everyone agreed. They drove up to the Gotham Hotel
and checked into two big rooms.
"I love the bars of soap," said Mickey.
"I love the big pillows," said Goofy.

curtain

screen

candy

wheelchair

seat

straw

cup

That night they went out and ate pizza for dinner. Then Mickey took everyone to a funny movie called *The Silliest Vacation Ever!*

Everybody laughed and laughed. "Our vacation is as silly as the one in the movie!" said Minnie with a giggle.

"And *we* get to eat popcorn," added Goofy.

scale

beach balls

shelf

box

tomato

bag

cash register

cart

wallet

The next morning Goofy drove the van to the supermarket so they could stock up on supplies for the beach. "Let's get more sandwiches, sodas, fruit, and chips," said Minnie.

"Can we get one of these beach balls?" asked Morty and Ferdie.

"Sure," said Mickey. "I can't wait to get to the beach."

They quickly finished shopping and then piled back into the van. Goofy drove and drove! Suddenly Pluto stuck his head out the window and began sniffing the air.

"I bet Pluto can smell the salty sea air!" said Goofy.

But soon they all saw what Pluto was sniffing…a field of corn on a farm!

cow

calf

goat

barbecue

pig

duck

rooster

sheep

chicken

egg

goose

hot dog

bow

fiddle

Mickey asked the farmer's wife, "Which way is it to the beach?"

"It's very far," she answered. "Why don't you spend the night here?"

"What a wonderful invitation!" said Minnie. "Thank you." The friends all leapt out of the van.

Mickey and Minnie helped milk the cows.

"Baa! Baa! Baa!" Morty and Ferdie said as they helped the farmer bring in the sheep.

Then they all prepared a barbecue, and Goofy played the fiddle so everybody could dance.

"Do-si-do!" he cried.

web

spider

mirror

clock

stair

railing

trunk

ladder

closet

ghost

skeleton

The next morning Mickey and his friends said good-
bye to the farmer and his wife.
"They told us the beach was this way," said Morty.
"No, no!" insisted Goofy. "I'm sure the farmer said the
other way." They drove and drove and drove down a
narrow road. At the end was a spooky house.
"Let's stop and explore. I love haunted houses," said
Morty as he ran ahead.
The others followed, but soon they heard a scream!
"Yipes! There's a ghost!" shrieked Ferdie.
"It's just Goofy in a sheet!" said Minnie with a laugh.
"We'd better get out of here," Mickey shouted, "before
Goofy scares anyone else!"

palm
tree

beach
umbrella

towel

shell

shovel

sand castle

pail

starfish

sea gull

boat

flippers

tube

oar

"Let's drive west this time," Mickey said. Very soon
they smelled the cool, salty ocean air. "Hurray! Hurray!
We've finally found the beach!" shouted Mickey.
Morty and Goofy ran and jumped into the ocean and
splashed and splashed and splashed!

haunted
house

city

dude
ranch

Two weeks after their zany vacation, Mickey invited
the gang over to look at his pictures from the trip.

"You know something?" marveled Minnie. "We had
more than one kind of vacation!"

"That's right," said Morty. "We saw a dude ranch and
camped in the woods; visited a town with a playground
and a big city, too; and stopped at a farm and a haunted
house!"

"I had a terrific time!" Goofy said, grinning. "Can I
drive again next year?"

"We'll think about it!" Mickey said, and everyone
laughed and laughed.

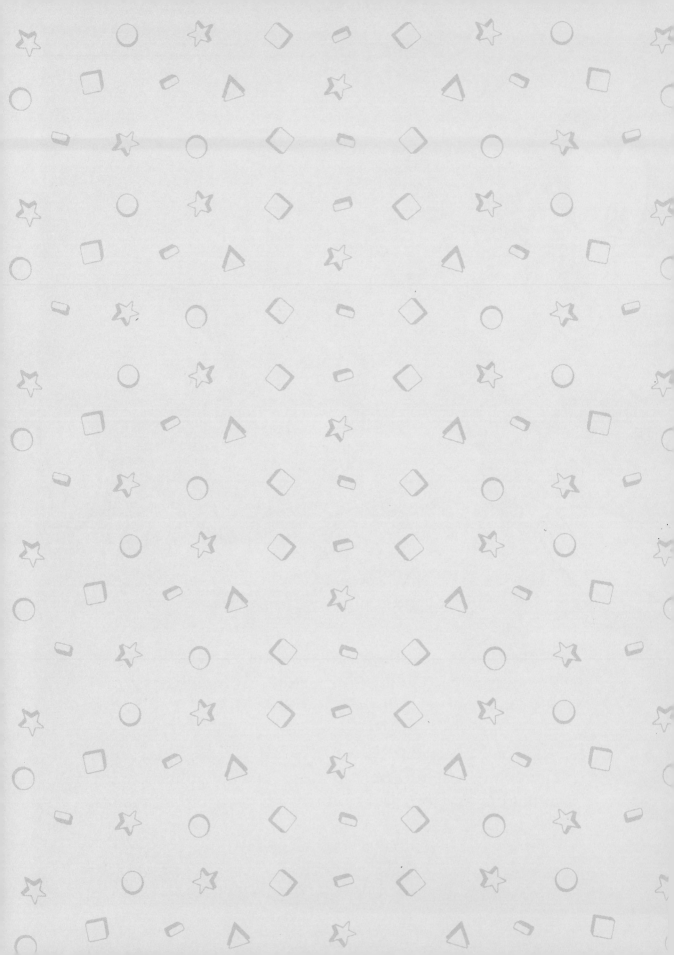